KU-458-644

Other books by Allan Ahlberg

A BIT MORE BERT

THE ADVENTURES OF BERT

The FAST FOX, SLOW DOG series (illus. André Amstutz)

FUNNYBONES: THE BLACK CAT (illus. André Amstutz)

FUNNYBONES: BUMPS IN THE NIGHT (illus. André Amstutz)

FUNNYBONES: DINOSAUR DREAMS (illus. André Amstutz)

FUNNYBONES: GIVE THE DOG A BONE (illus. André Amstutz)

FUNNYBONES: THE PET SHOP (illus. André Amstutz)

The HAPPY FAMILIES series (illus. various)

THE LITTLE CAT BABY

Other books by Janet and Allan Ahlberg

THE BABY'S CATALOGUE

BURGLAR BILL

BYE BYE BABY

THE CLOTHES HORSE AND OTHER STORIES

COPS AND ROBBERS

EACH PEACH PEAR PLUM

FUNNYBONES

IT WAS A DARK AND STORMY NIGHT

JEREMIAH IN THE DARK WOODS

THE JOLLY CHRISTMAS POSTMAN

THE JOLLY POSTMAN

THE JOLLY POCKET POSTMAN

PEEPO!

STARTING SCHOOL

Skeleton Crew

ALLAN AHLBERG • ANDRÉ AMSTUTZ

PUFFIN

On a dark dark night,
on a dark dark sea,
in a dark dark boat
three skeletons float . . .

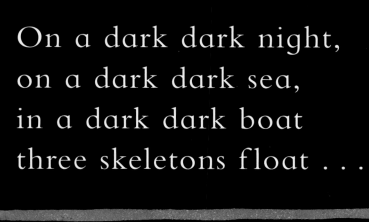

on a holiday.

The big one is dozing
in his deckchair.
"Zzz!"

The dog one is dozing
in his hammock.
"Zzz!"
The little one is fishing.

. . . and it throws *him* back.

Splash!

The next night
in the dark boat
under the starry sky
the big one has a try.

The big skeleton catches a little fish
and throws it back.
He catches a big fish and keeps it.
He catches a bigger fish . . .

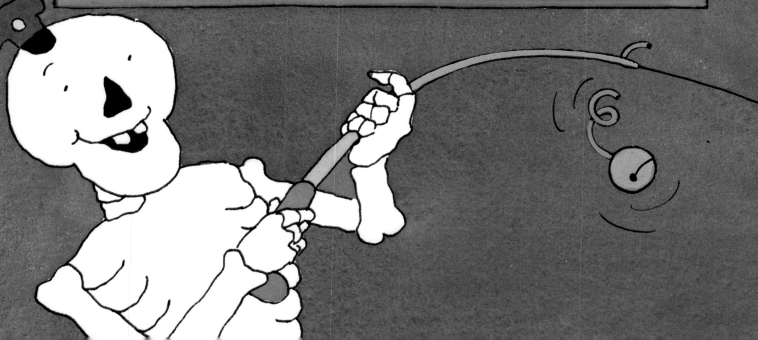

And – "Yo – ho – ho!" –
the *pirates* come.

The pirates climb aboard
looking for treasure.
They steal the deckchair
and the hammock.

They steal the fishing rod
and the catfish.
"Miaow!"
They steal . . . the boat!

The next night . . .
nothing happens.

But the *next* night,
under a starry sky
and over the deep blue sea,
the skeletons spy . . . a tree.
"Yippee!"

On the island
the big skeleton
finds a parrot.
"Pretty Polly!"

The next night a lot happens.
A storm blows up.
The thunder crashes,
the lightning flashes,
the wind howls
and the dog howls too.
"Howl!"

As quick as a blink
the raft is blown
across the foam . . .

The End (or is it?)

The End

PUFFIN BOOKS

UK | USA | Canada | Ireland | Australia
India | New Zealand | South Africa

Puffin Books is part of the Penguin Random House group of companies
whose addresses can be found at global.penguinrandomhouse.com.

www.penguin.co.uk   www.puffin.co.uk   www.ladybird.co.uk

First published by William Heinemann Ltd 1992
First published in Puffin Books 2005
This edition published 2018

001

Text copyright © Allan Ahlberg, 1992
Illustrations copyright © André Amstutz, 1992
All rights reserved

The moral right of the author and illustrator has been asserted

Printed in China
A CIP catalogue record for this book is available from the British Library

ISBN: 978–0–241–37768–0

All correspondence to:
Puffin Books, Penguin Random House Children's
80 Strand, London WC2R 0RL

MIX
Paper from
responsible sources
FSC® C018179